— For my dear friends, with love. Special thanks also to Manli Peng and Kate Wilson whose help and encouragement was greatly appreciated. W.M.

— To Susan Hou, for all her help. R.K.

Illustrations copyright © 1998 by Wenhai Ma
English text copyright © 1998 by Robert Kraus
Chinese text copyright © 1998 by Debby Chen

Published in the United States of America by
Pan Asian Publications (USA) Inc.
29564 Union City Blvd., Union City, CA 94587

Tel. (510) 475-1185   Fax (510) 475-1489

ISBN 1-57227-043-8
Library of Congress Catalog Card Number: 97-80532

Editorial and production assistance: William Mersereau, Art & Publishing Consultants

Printed in Hong Kong

THE MAKING of
MONKEY KING

Retold by Robert Kraus and Debby Chen
Illustrated by Wenhai Ma

Pan Asian Publications

Long, long ago, by the far eastern land of Ao-lai was a great sea. And out of this swirling sea rose Flower Fruit Mountain. At the top of this mountain lay a giant mysterious rock.

For millions of years, the rock had soaked up the light from the sun and moon until one day, it burst right open! And out jumped a small stone monkey!

The very first thing he did was bow to the four directions — east, south, west and north. As he did so, two golden beams shot from his eyes and pierced the sky, startling the Jade Emperor living in Heavenly Palace.

The Emperor quickly called his two captains,
Thousand Mile Eye and Fair Wind Ear, to investigate.
They threw open the South Gate of Heaven, spotted the
stone monkey, and quickly reported back to the Jade
Emperor who merely nodded, saying, "Since all
creatures on earth are magical, this stone monkey
should really be no surprise to us."

The stone monkey soon joined the other monkeys who lived on the mountain. Together they spent many joyful days frolicking among wild flowers and feasting on fruit. One hot day, the monkeys went to bathe in a cool, rushing stream. Restless and curious as ever, they all decided to find out where the stream began.

The monkeys swung from tree to tree, following the twists and turns of the stream. Finally, they discovered a giant waterfall hanging like a great white curtain from the sky. "The first one to jump through this waterfall and return safely," declared the monkeys, "will become our king." The stone monkey pushed his way through the crowd and shouted, "I will go!" He closed his eyes and leaped.

When he opened his eyes, he saw a splendid iron bridge stretching before him. Beside the bridge was an inscription that read: *Flower Fruit Mountain is Blessed, and Water Curtain Cave Leads to Heaven.*

Walking boldly over the bridge, the stone monkey soon found a great cave. Inside, there were stone chairs and beds, and hundreds of stone bowls and pots. "What a perfect place to live!" he thought, and he raced back to fetch his friends. Eagerly, they followed him back through the waterfall.

The stone monkey seated himself on the biggest chair.
Raising a paw, he declared, "We agreed that whoever
jumped through the falls shall be king. So now you
must salute me!"

"Hurrah! Long live the Handsome Monkey King!"
cheered the rest of the monkeys.

Life was now better than ever! During the day they
played on Flower Fruit Mountain, and during the night
they slept in Water Curtain Cave. They no longer
worried about harsh weather or fearsome beasts!

For four hundred years they lived this carefree life,
until one day, during a jolly banquet, a sad thought
struck Monkey King and he suddenly burst into tears.
"Why are you crying, your Majesty?" asked the
bewildered monkeys. "Isn't our life wonderful?"

"Life is wonderful," wailed Monkey King, "but one day
I will die and this wonderful life will be all over!"

Upon hearing this, all the other monkeys burst into
tears as well. Finally, a wise old gibbon came forward.
"Never fear," he said, "I have heard that Buddhas,
Immortals and Sages are not subject to Yama, the God
of Death. Why not find these great beings and ask
them for the secret to eternal life?"

Monkey King was overjoyed! The very next day
he said good-bye to the other monkeys and set
out on his journey in a tiny raft.

He sailed in and out of sunny days and moonlit nights until he came to a small seaside village. Some fishermen were on the beach, salting their catch. Monkey King noticed with envy that they all wore clothes. He jumped up and down and made such awful faces that all the fishermen ran away in fright. In his haste, one fisherman ran right out of his clothes!

This suited the cheeky monkey just fine. He dressed himself in the clothes and set off into the land of humans, proud as a peacock.

Monkey King traveled for many years, asking everyone he met if they knew the whereabouts of a Buddha, an Immortal, or even a Sage. But no one knew. Then one day, he happened upon a woodcutter at the edge of a forest. The woodcutter told him that, indeed, he knew of a magical Immortal named Master Subodhi who lived in a nearby cave with his many students.

The Master, strange to say, seemed to be expecting
Monkey King. And wasting no time, Monkey King
asked him if he could become his student. Subodhi
looked deeply into his face and replied, "I know you
are sincere, and that you have traveled far to find me,
but I see also that you are vain and naughty!"

"Oh no, I'm not!" protested the Monkey King,
"Please, give me a chance!"

Subodhi finally relented, "Very well," he said,
"you may be my student. While you study with
me, you will be known as *Sun Wukong*."*

*Aware-of-Nothingness

Monkey King lived humbly like the other students. He listened intently to Subodhi's teachings and learned the martial arts. Seven long years passed, but he was still no closer to learning the secret for eternal life. Monkey King could stand it no longer. One day, in the middle of a class, he jumped up and cried, "This is just too boring! I have been here so long and all I have learned to do is clean, cook and wash." Master Subodhi was furious! He stepped off the podium and struck Monkey King three times with his ruler. "You don't want to learn this! You don't want to learn that!" he said, "What do you want to learn?" With that, Master Subodhi left the room, hands crossed behind his back.

At three o'clock the next morning, Monkey King entered Master Subodhi's cave through the back door and knelt beside his bed. Suddenly awakened, Subodhi cried, "What are you doing here?" Monkey King replied, "When you struck me on the head three times, that was a sign that I must visit you at three o'clock. And when you put your hands behind your back, that was a sign that I must come in through the back door."

Monkey King understood the secret signs! Master Subodhi decided that he was indeed ready to learn the Immortal Secrets. He whispered the sacred verses into Monkey King's ear, then sent him back to his own cave to practice. Three years later, Subodhi also taught him the Seventy-Two Transformations. Now, he could change into almost anything!

One evening, when everyone was out admiring the new moon, Subodhi asked Monkey King how his studies were going. "Very well," he replied, "I've already mastered the art of cloud-soaring." Trying to impress his master, he flew into the clouds, traveled four miles and was back in a wink.

"That was not cloud-soaring," laughed Subodhi, "that was only cloud crawling! Real cloud-soaring means you can fly a thousand miles with one jump!"

"That's impossible!" cried Monkey King.

"Nothing is impossible, only the mind makes it so," replied Subodhi. He leaned forward and whispered the spell for cloud-soaring. In no time, Monkey King mastered it.

Although Subodhi was pleased with Monkey King, he often saw flashes of cockiness. He warned Monkey King: "Never show off your powers, or they will get you in trouble." Monkey King promised he would not. But one day, while playing about with some students, Monkey King transformed himself into a pine tree, flaunting his powers. The ruckus brought Subodhi running from his cave. One look at the pine tree and he realized what had happened. "You broke your promise," Subodhi cried angrily. "Leave my cave!"

Monkey King pleaded for another chance, but Subodhi would not be persuaded. "When you show off, people will ask you for the secret. Bad people will use it to harm others. And if you refuse to share your secrets, you could be harmed yourself. You have been here twenty years, and that is enough. Go back to your kingdom and use your powers to do good deeds."

Although sad, Monkey King thanked his master for everything, recited the cloud-soaring spell, and flew off. In a twinkling, he was back at his beloved Flower Fruit Mountain.

How strange that no one was there to greet him. He went to Water Curtain Cave and found everything lying in a broken heap. In a corner lay an old monkey who sobbed, "While you were away, Demon of Chaos came and took everyone away. I was so sick, they left me behind." Monkey King was furious, and he flew off to the Demon's cave.

"Come on out, Demon of Chaos!" Monkey King shouted. Hearing the challenge, the Demon quickly charged out of his cave, but seeing only a small monkey in front of him, he burst out laughing. How could one monkey fight a fearsome demon and his villainous crew?

But in less than a blink of an eye, Monkey King flashed through the air, landing a stinging punch on the Demon's nose!

Now in a rage, the Demon swung his sword at Monkey King who easily dodged it by flying into a tree. Again the Demon swung and missed, but this time his sword dug deep into the tree trunk. Try as he might, he could not budge it! Monkey King plucked a bit of his fur, recited a spell, and the hairs changed into an army of small monkeys. Swarming over the Demon, they held him down and tied him up with magic ropes. With a great push, they sent him rolling down the mountainside.

After chasing off the other villains, Monkey King recited the spell again, and the little monkeys changed back into hairs. He hurried to the Demon's cave and released all his friends.

"Hurrah to our amazing Monkey King!" they cheered. Monkey King summoned the clouds, and carried his friends back to Water Curtain Cave. They celebrated their freedom and the return of their king with feasting and dancing for three days and three nights.

It was a glorious return for the Monkey King! But this, dear friends, is really just the beginning of many more adventures…

The Monkey King

In the seventh century, during the Tang dynasty, a Chinese Buddhist priest named Xuan Zang (c. 596-664) embarked on a dangerous pilgrimage to India to bring Buddhist scriptures back to China. The entire journey lasted twenty years. The priest returned to China in 645 bearing some six hundred texts and devoted the rest of his life to translating these into Chinese. In addition, he dictated a travelogue to a disciple and called it *The Tang Record of the Western Territories*. In it, he recounted details from his journey, the people he had met, and the harsh geography he survived (he scaled three of Asia's highest mountain ranges and nearly died of thirst on the desert plains).

Xuan Zang became a favorite of the Tang Emperor and a famous religious folk hero. For the next one thousand years the story of his pilgrimage inspired the literary imagination of storytellers and writers who embellished the journey with unbelievable episodes and fantastic characters drawn from popular folklore. In the thirteenth century, a supernatural monkey and pig became the priest's travel companions. Some scholars believe that the monkey may have been derived from Hanumat, the Monkey King from the Hindu tale, *Ramayana*. In the fourteenth century, a stage play in twenty-four scenes was composed. This drama is important because it contains all the main themes that would later appear in the sixteenth century Ming dynasty epic narrative *Journey to the West*.

Although written anonymously, there is much evidence showing that *Journey to the West* was most likely written around 1575 by a court official, poet and humor writer named Wu Cheng'en (c. 1500-82). The work is a massive, hundred-chapter masterpiece, and is more elaborate than any of the journey tales that came before it. It is not a novel in the conventional sense, but rather a complex narrative of episodic stories held together by the journey, its unifying motif. Wu Cheng'en did not merely weave the myriad tales together, he created a sophisticated allegory rich with humor, action, philosophy and satire. The mythical Monkey King who wreaks havoc in heaven, hell and everything in between, occupies the entire first part of Wu's epic. These first seven chapters are devoted to the beginnings of the Monkey King before his journey west: his birth and rise to kingship, his acquisition of magic under Master Subodhi, his gaining of immortality and disturbance of Heaven, and finally, his imprisonment under a mountain—the punishment set by the Buddha for his insolence. Throughout the remainder of the legend he consistently upstages the priest with his robust character and colorful antics.